Damage

Robin Stevenson

orca soundings

ORCA BOOK PUBLISHERS

F I C
S T E

Copyright © 2013 Robin Stevenson

Library and Archives Canada Cataloguing in Publication

Stevenson, Robin, 1968-
Damage / Robin Stevenson.
(Orca soundings)

Issued also in electronic formats.
ISBN 978-1-4598-0363-3 (bound).--ISBN 978-1-4598-0360-2 (pbk.)

I. Title. II. Series: Orca soundings
PS8637.T487D36 2013   jC813'.6   C2012-907480-2

First published in the United States, 2013
Library of Congress Control Number: 2012952957

Summary: What starts out as a harmless road trip
becomes a desperate search for the truth.

*Orca Book Publishers is dedicated to preserving the environment and has printed
this book on Forest Stewardship Council® certified paper.*

Orca Book Publishers gratefully acknowledges the support for its publishing
programs provided by the following agencies: the Government of Canada through
the Canada Book Fund and the Canada Council for the Arts,
and the Province of British Columbia through the BC Arts Council
and the Book Publishing Tax Credit.

Cover photography by Getty Images

ORCA BOOK PUBLISHERS
PO Box 5626, Stn. B
Victoria, BC Canada
V8R 6S4

ORCA BOOK PUBLISHERS
PO Box 468
Custer, WA USA
98240-0468

www.orcabook.com
Printed and bound in Canada.

16 15 14 13 • 4 3 2 1

Chapter One

From where I sat, the view was pretty sweet. Above me was a wide-open sky without even a trace of a cloud. In front of me, the pool shimmered cool, clear and blue. To my left, a line of palm trees bordered the motel courtyard. All very California—but none of it compared with the view to my right. From behind the mirrored lenses of my sunglasses,

I sneaked yet another peek at the most beautiful girl I had ever seen.

I kid you not. This girl was dazzling in a way that no one is dazzling in real life. She looked Photoshopped. Her wet hair was slicked back from her face, a white towel was draped across her tanned shoulders, and her long bare legs were stretched out in front of her. There was something oddly familiar about her. Maybe she was a famous actress or a model or something... though you wouldn't expect to find a famous person at a cheap highway motel. Whoever she was, she was breathtaking. And there she was, in a red bikini, sitting three plastic lounge chairs away from me.

Too bad the two chairs between us were occupied by the reclining, swim-suit-clad bodies of my mother and father.

I heard a splash behind me and turned around. A dark-haired toddler was holding an upside-down red bucket and staring at me solemnly. I smiled at him, and his eyes opened a little wider, but he didn't say anything.

I looked around for a parental figure but didn't see one. "Nice red bucket," I said. Lame, I knew, but I didn't have much experience with kids.

"Mmm," he agreed and then delivered a long speech that I couldn't understand. He might have said something about unicorns, or possibly raisins, but I wasn't sure.

"Where's your mom?" I was no expert on these things, but I was pretty sure he was too little to be at the pool by himself.

"Sorry. Is he bothering you?" The girl from three chairs over sat up and beckoned to him. "Come here, Zach."

"No. I mean, it's fine. He's fine," I stammered. "I mean, he's not bothering me. He was just telling me about

3

his bucket. I think. Though he might have been saying something about raisins." I sounded like an idiot. *Shut up, Theo, shut up*.

"Ah. Raisins, huh?" She smiled, her lips parting to reveal white teeth.

She had a slight overbite, which only the son of a dentist would notice. Even on vacation, Dad was compelled to point out every dental defect he observed. Not that *her* overbite was a defect. It suited her perfectly. As did her dark hair. And her full lips. And the dimple in her left cheek.

"Mmm," I said. If I kept my mouth shut, I couldn't say anything stupid, right?

"Zachy, did you want raisins?" She reached for a bag under her chair. "Are you hungry, Zach? Time for a snack?"

"Raisins," he said.

"He's *yours*?" I couldn't believe she had a kid. So much for my fantasy that

4

we might hook up—not that there'd been any real hope of that anyway.

"I was watching him." There was an edge to her voice. "I watch him all the time when we're at the pool."

"I didn't think you weren't," I said quickly. "Um, you just don't look like a mom, that's all."

She was still glaring at me. God, she looked familiar. I just couldn't place where I'd seen her before. TV, maybe. She had to be someone famous.

"And what exactly does a mom look like?" she asked.

"I don't...I didn't mean...it's not like I think there's anything wrong with being a mom," I said. "Just, you know, I thought you were my age. And I think of moms as, you know, older. Arrgh. Sorry." I groaned, stood up and took off my sunglasses. "Can I start over? Please?"

She raised one dark eyebrow.

"I'm Theo. And that's my mom and dad right there." I pointed at them. They were both out cold, and Dad was snoring softly. "See? Way older."

She laughed. "Ronnie," she said. "And I'm twenty-two."

"Yeah? Nice to meet you." Should I add a couple of years and say I was nineteen? Maybe she wouldn't ask. "So, um, Ronnie…" Gears turned in some rusty part of my brain and something clicked, slid into place. "Oh my god. *Ronnie?* Ronnie *Gleeson?*"

She stared at me, eyes wide.

"Theo Dimitropolous," I said. "You're from Portland, right? You used to…" I trailed off.

"Babysit you!" She crowed. "Theo! Holy crap. I can't believe this. Look at you."

"Yeah, well…" I grabbed my damp towel from the lounger behind me and wrapped it around my waist.

"You were, like, ten years old the last time I saw you."

My face was on fire. "Yeah. Eleven, actually." I'd been a nerdy kid obsessed with *Star Wars*, making stop-motion animation movies with my LEGO Millennium Falcon. My earliest fantasies had all been about Ronnie. Back then, I would've traded my whole *Star Wars* action-figure set for one glimpse of Ronnie in the bikini she was wearing right now.

"I can't believe this." She shook her head slowly, staring at me.

I hoped she wasn't picturing me in my R2-D2 pajamas. "You moved away, right?"

"Yeah, after grade eleven." She made a face. "I finished high school in Seattle."

"I remember that. I was so bummed out when you left."

"Well, you didn't really need a baby-sitter anymore." She looked over at my parents, snoring on their loungers. "I didn't even recognize your folks. Are you guys on vacation?"

"Yeah, sort of. We're going to visit my brother. He lives near Santa Rosa."

"I don't think I ever met him," she says.

"He'd already moved out. He's ten years older than me," I said.

"Raisins," Zach said.

"Right." Ronnie scooped him up with one arm. "Come on, little guy. We better get you dressed before you get cold."

I picked up her bag. "Do you need a hand or anything?"

She took the bag from me. "I'm fine. But thanks, Theo. I'll see you around."

"Yeah," I said. "Great. I mean, I hope so."

And then I watched Ronnie carry her squirming toddler out of the pool area and around the corner, out of sight.

Chapter Two

We ate dinner that evening in the motel restaurant. I was still daydreaming about Ronnie. Mom and Dad were grumpy from their pre-dinner nap. Not that they hadn't been grumpy before. The three of us had been arguing since we left Portland. In fact, we'd been pretty much locked into one long argument for the last couple of months, ever since my buddy Koli got busted selling pot at school. My parents refused to believe that I wasn't involved, and I refused to stop hanging out with him. Koli and I had been best buds since sixth grade. Sure, he'd screwed up, but I wasn't about to drop him.

"Everything on this menu is deep-fried," Dad complained. "Fish and chips, fried chicken, onion rings..."

"Mmm. Onion rings." My favorite.

"Look at this," he grumbled. "Even the salad has tortilla chips on it."

"So ask for it without the chips," I said.

He just grunted.

Mom peered into the mirror on the wall beside our table. "I'm sunburned! Look at this." She tapped her nose and then her forehead before turning to frown at my father. "You might have woken me up instead of letting me lie there getting skin cancer."

"Don't exaggerate," Dad said. "You're barely even pink."

"Dad was asleep too," I said. "Out cold. Maybe you guys should skip the happy-hour drinks, huh?"

Dad snorted. "I wasn't sleeping. I just closed my eyes for a few minutes."

"You were snoring like a freight train." I kept glancing over to the restaurant entrance, hoping that Ronnie and Zach would make an appearance. I hated the thought that I might not see her again. "So, I guess we have to hit the road bright and early, huh?"

"Your brother's expecting us for lunch," Mom said. "We should be on the road by nine at the latest. Breakfast, pack up, head out."

My brother. Darrell Junior, following in Dad's footsteps like a good son. At twenty-seven, Darrell had graduated from dentistry and was already middle-aged. He lived with his wife in a four-bedroom house in the suburbs of Santa Rosa and had just joined a family dental practice where he fixed rich kids' cavities while they watched cartoons on TV screens set into the ceiling.

"You won't believe who I just ran into," I said.

"Who?" Mom took a sip of her water, eyeing me over the rim of her glass.

"Ronnie Gleeson. Remember? She used to babysit me."

Dad raised his eyebrows. "The Gleesons. I remember them. I used to golf with Patrick. They moved to Port Townsend, didn't they?"

"Seattle."

"She was a lovely girl," Mom said. "You had such a crush on her, Theo." She sighed sadly, like she missed the good old days when I was eleven years old and she didn't have to worry that I was turning into a drug addict.

"Yeah, yeah." I lifted my water glass and set it down again, making overlapping water rings on the table.

"So how is she? What's she doing here?"

"Fine. She's on vacation, I guess. She looks good. Got a kid now."

"Really? She's a bit young, isn't she?"

"No," I said sharply, even though I'd thought the same thing. "She's twenty-two. And her kid's really little, just a toddler."

"Well, you should've invited them to join us for dinner." Mom fanned herself with the menu. "Phew. I can't take this heat. Thank God your brother has a pool."

"Yeah," I said. "Thank God Darrell's perfect."

She gave me a look. "Don't start, Theo."

I stared down at the menu. "Can I get a Corona?" I was pretty sure I already knew the answer, but what the hell—we were on holiday, right?

"Theo…" Mom frowned.

Dad gave me a steel-eyed glare. "Sure you can. In four years, when you're legal drinking age. You start drinking now, you're breaking the law."

"Take off those sunglasses, Theo," Mom said. "You're in a restaurant."

I took them off.

Dad put his elbows on the table and leaned forward so that his face was inches from mine. "Your eyes are very bloodshot."

"Chlorine," I said. "I was in the pool, remember?"

"Hmmm." He didn't move.

"Dad, are you trying to smell my breath?" I blew at him. "Here. How's that? Doritos, extra cheesy."

"Don't get smart with me, young man. We're just looking out for you." He sat back. "Marijuana kills motivation. You smoke that stuff, you'll go nowhere."

I wasn't into anything harder than an occasional cold beer, but I was tired of trying to convince them of that. "I'm not smoking anything and I don't want to go anywhere," I said irritably.

"Look at Koli," Mom says. "He got into drugs and he's having to face the music now. Is that what you want?"

I rolled my eyes. "All I want is to eat dinner without you two getting on my case. All right?"

"On your case?" Dad repeated. "*On your case?* What the heck is that supposed to mean?"

"Maybe Darrell can talk to him," Mom said in a low voice, as if I wasn't sitting right there.

That did it. I stood up.

"You know what?" I said. "You're right. This restaurant does suck." And I stormed out, leaving them opening and shutting their mouths like a pair of goldfish.

Chapter Three

I had cut across the courtyard and was heading toward my room when I saw Ronnie, sitting on the cement walkway near the pool. She'd changed into denim shorts and a white T-shirt with a big pink flower on it, and she had a stroller beside her. I grinned at her, my bad mood vanishing like fog in sunshine. "Hey, Ronnie. Where are you off to?"

"Nowhere." She leaned against the brick wall. "I've been walking around for an hour, trying to get Zachy to go to sleep."

I looked at Zach. He had a glazed look on his face, and his thumb was firmly planted in his mouth. "Can I get you anything? I mean, if you're hungry or..." I trailed off.

"I'm fine. We've got food in the car. It's easier than taking Zach to restaurants. And cheaper."

"Right." I leaned against the wall too. Heat radiated from the bricks. "So, we're leaving in the morning."

"To see your brother, right? That's nice."

"No, actually. It sucks. It'll be three days of all of them ganging up to convince me to quit smoking pot and

study hard so that I can be a dentist."
I groaned and rubbed my hands across
my face. "And I don't even smoke pot."

She laughed out loud. "And do you
want to be a dentist?"

"God, no." I made a face. "I can't
think of anything more disgusting.
Sticking your fingers in people's
mouths, seeing all the little bits of food
stuck in their teeth, scraping off plaque
and poking around..." I shuddered.
"Just the thought makes me gag."

"So what do you want to do?"
Ronnie's voice was low, and she sounded
amused.

"I don't know." I didn't want her
to think I was still a dumb kid with a
dumb dream.

"Come on. You must have some
idea."

"Nah."

She laughed. "Liar. Spit it out—I
won't laugh."

"Yeah, okay. I guess I like film. It'd be cool to make movies. Direct them, maybe, or just work on them."

"Ha! Remember how you used to make those little videos? With your action figures? Obi-Wan Kenobi and Yoda…"

"Yeah. And Han Solo." I lowered my voice. *"Hokey religions and ancient weapons are no match for a good blaster at your side, kid."*

Ronnie laughed out loud. "He was always my favorite."

"Yeah, he had the best lines." I decided not to mention that I knew most of them by heart.

"So you want to make movies for real, huh? That's cool."

I shrugged. "Dunno how realistic it is."

"Lots of people do it." She stuck her hands into her shorts pockets. "You should come with me and Zachy.

We're leaving as soon as I can get him to go to sleep. Driving down to Los Angeles. Ten hours, and you could be in Hollywood, baby."

I stared at her. Was she kidding? She had to be kidding.

"I'm serious," she said, as if I had spoken aloud. "I'd love the company. We could split the driving."

"You're leaving tonight?"

"Yeah, we're checked out already. Our bags have been in the lobby since lunchtime. I know it seems weird, but Zach hates being in his car seat, and if I travel at night, there's more chance that he'll sleep."

"I don't know…"

"Come on, it'd be fun. I've got a friend in LA who's been in movies. She knows all kinds of people. I bet she could hook you up with a job."

My heart was pounding hard and fast, and my mouth was suddenly dry.

Some choice—drive with my parents to see Darrell and get some sense talked into me, or drive to Hollywood with Ronnie, aka the Most Beautiful Girl in the World.

"I can't just take off on my parents," I said. Though really, I thought, why shouldn't I? They'd done nothing but nag me and accuse me of lying since we'd left home the day before.

"I didn't mean you should run away." She laughed. "Jeez, give me some credit."

"You mean, ask them?"

"Yeah, doofus," she said. "Ask them. And hurry up." She nodded at Zach. "He's finally conked out, which means I can put him in his car seat without a total meltdown."

Ronnie obviously didn't remember my parents very well. There was no way in hell that they would agree. On the other hand, I couldn't imagine letting this opportunity slip away.

I could just do it without asking. Just go, right now. There'd be nothing my folks could do about it. They'd freak out, sure, but that wouldn't be my problem if I wasn't here.

They wouldn't even be able to call to yell at me, since I no longer had a phone. I'd made the mistake of lending it to Koli at a party a couple of weeks ago, and somehow—I wasn't clear on the details—it had taken a fatal dive into a toilet.

I took a deep breath. "Sure," I said. "I'll go ask."

I headed toward the restaurant, but as soon as I was out of Ronnie's sight, I ducked into a restroom and waited for a few minutes. Then I headed back to Ronnie, a smile on my face, and gave her a thumbs-up. "Go figure," I said. "They said yes. I think they must be tired of arguing with me." I couldn't quite meet her eyes, and I hoped she wouldn't notice. "Um, yeah. So I'll just grab my things."

Ronnie smiled widely, her cheeks dimpling under her oversized sunglasses. Her teeth looked startlingly white in her suntanned face. "Awesome, Theo."

God, I loved the way she said my name. I slipped into the hotel room, grabbed a pen and paper from the desk and started to scrawl a note for my parents. I wanted to tell them I was tired of being compared to Darrell, tired of being nagged about school, tired of them not trusting me, but I didn't know where to begin. Finally, I just wrote, *Mom, Dad. Don't worry, I'm fine. Decided to travel with Ronnie for a few days. Have a good visit with D. I'll be in touch.*

I quickly packed, slung my duffel bag over one shoulder and headed to the parking lot. Ronnie was standing beside her car, a wide-brimmed hat shading her face and a disposable cup in each hand. "Free coffee from the lobby. From the taste, I don't think it's actually meant for human consumption."

"Uh, thanks?" I took one from her, though coffee was the last thing I needed. There was so much adrenaline rushing through me, I felt shaky and almost sick.

Ronnie laughed. "Think of it as fuel." She took off the hat, tossed it into the backseat and shook her hair loose. "Let's do it, Theo. Let's hit the road."

Chapter Four

Zach was buckled into his car seat, still fast asleep. With the heavy-duty straps over his shoulders and across his chest, he looked like a little astronaut about to blast off.

"I can't believe I'm doing this," I said.

Ronnie grinned at me. "It'll be nice to have company. Zach's great, but let's face it, he has a pretty limited range of conversation topics."

"I bet he doesn't do his share of the driving either."

"Ha. He'd love to. He adores anything with wheels."

I buckled my seat belt and glanced over my shoulder at him. "Is he always such a good sleeper?"

She hesitated before answering. "I guess so—I mean, yeah. He is."

"What's wrong?" I studied the frown lines that had appeared between her eyebrows.

"Nothing." Ronnie started the engine. "Let's go."

Last chance to change your mind. I closed my eyes for a moment, imagining the shock on my parents' faces when they got back to the hotel room and realized I'd taken off. Dad would be furious with me. Mom, too, but she'd take it out on Dad, blaming him.

If you hadn't insisted on sniffing his breath at dinner, this would never have happened. You never know when to back off, do you?

Nope, I didn't need to listen to any more of their arguments. "Right," I said. "Hollywood, here we come."

Zach slept for the first twenty minutes and then woke up crying. We were just outside Redding, heading south on I-5, but Ronnie pulled over and tried to comfort him. She offered snacks, books, toys, but Zach just kept screaming at the top of his lungs. At least, I sure hoped it was his top—any louder, and he'd do permanent damage to my hearing. Ronnie unbuckled him and tried to pick him up, but he just kicked his legs, arched his back and tried to push her away. She looked like she was about to start crying herself.

"Maybe we should just keep driving," I said at last. "Buckle him back in and keep going, you know? I mean, if he's just going to scream anyway."

Ronnie gave me a look, like I was a terrible person for suggesting it, but she stuck him back in his car seat. You can only park at the side of the high-way listening to a toddler screaming for so long.

"How about I drive?" I suggested. "You can sit with him."

She nodded. "Jump to lightspeed," she said. "Though my car starts to rattle if you go over sixty, so maybe not."

I dropped my voice an octave and did a Han Solo swagger, smacking the car roof with the palm of my hand. "She may not look like much, but she's got it where it counts, kid."

Ronnie shook her head as she slipped into the backseat beside Zach. "Un-freaking-believable."

I drove and Zach cried. He yelled and sobbed until his whole face was covered with bright red blotches.

"Um, Theo? Yesterday in the car, singing really helped," Ronnie said.

"Singing? Me? I can't sing." I glanced at her face in the rearview mirror and caught her wiping tears from her cheeks. I groaned. "Okay, okay," I said. "We'll sing."

After a few verses, Zach settled down, but each time we tried to stop singing, he went right back to screaming. When we passed the exit for Clear Lake—the turnoff that I should've been taking with my parents, to go to Darrell's place in Santa Rosa—my stomach started doing flips. God, my parents were going to freak out. What had I been thinking?

Ronnie and I sang Raffi songs non-stop all the way to Sacramento—over two straight hours. *"Baby Beluga in the deep blue sea…"* My eyes met Ronnie's in the rearview mirror and she gave me a weak smile. She'd stopped crying, at least. I kept singing. *"Swim so wild and you swim so free…"*

This was so not what I had imagined when I pictured the two of us driving off into the sunset together.

Just past Sacramento, I heard sirens close behind us. I glanced in the rearview mirror. Cops. I was over the limit but only just. "Seriously?" I muttered.

"Oh my god." Ronnie's voice was strained. "Oh my *god*, Theo. Were you speeding? Damn it, what were you thinking? Do you have any idea—"

"I'm only, like, five miles over," I protested. "If that. I mean, cars are flying past me in the other lane." I slowed down and started to pull over.

"I can't believe this," she said, her voice rising. "I shouldn't have let you drive."

"What's the big deal?" I drove onto the shoulder, braking. "If we get a ticket, I'll pay it, okay? So chill."

"I don't care about a goddamn *ticket*," she said. Zach started to cry again. "Shut up, Zach!" Ronnie turned to him and grabbed his shoulders. "Goddamn it! Zach, please. Just stop crying."

I got an icy feeling in the pit of my stomach. I stopped the car and turned to look over my shoulder at her. "Please tell me the car isn't stolen."

"Theo! Of course it's not *stolen*."

"What is it then? Why are you freaking out?" Behind me, I could see the cop getting out of his car and walking toward us. My chest tightened. "Ronnie? Is there something I should know?"

Zach started crying louder than ever. "Just don't use my name," Ronnie said. She unbuckled Zach and pulled him out of his car seat and onto her lap.

I had started to roll down my window, and the cop was only a few feet away. "*What?* Are you serious?"

"Or Zach's," she said under her breath.

The car was stolen. I just knew it. My hands were slick with sweat. I wiped them on my jeans and turned to watch the cop walk the last few feet to our car.

Ronnie was cooing to Zach now. "Come here, baby. I'm sorry I yelled at you. You want a snack, honey? Raisins? Goldfish crackers?" She rummaged in the bag on the seat beside her.

I felt sick. Sure, Ronnie had been my babysitter—but that was six years ago, when she was an eleventh-grader. I knew nothing about this girl sitting behind me. She could be anyone.

A car thief. Or worse, a drug dealer. What if the trunk was full of coke or something?

God knows my parents weren't going to believe that I had nothing to do with it.

"Good evening," the cop said, leaning down to the open window.

"Um, hi. Sorry. Was I speeding? I thought I was pretty much going the speed limit." My heart was racing, and I had to fight to keep my voice level. *Please, God, I know I haven't been to church in a few years, but if you could just do me this one favor and not let him look in the trunk…*

The cop was middle-aged, dark-eyed and brown-skinned, with a heavy moustache. I figured he was leaning in to check my breath, like my father always did. "You had anything to drink tonight?" he asked.

"No." I gestured at the paper cups in the drinks tray. "Just coffee."

"Oregon license plates, huh? Where are you heading?"

"I'm from Portland. Going to Los Angeles. Um, I have family down there," I said. It wasn't true, but it seemed like a good thing to say. Like, a responsible kind of reason to be driving through California at night. *Please don't look in the trunk. Don't search the car.* "Um, was I over the speed limit?"

He straightened up with a grunt, hands on his lower back. "You weren't speeding. You've got a taillight out though."

"Oh. I didn't realize..."

"No one ever does. No one thinks to check their taillights." He shook his head. "Better get that fixed, all right?"

"Yeah, for sure. Thanks for letting me know." Zach wasn't crying anymore, and I didn't want to draw attention to him and Ronnie in the backseat, so I kept my eyes on the cop. "I'll get that dealt with right away."

"All right then. You have a safe trip."

"Thanks." My hand was shaking as I rolled my window closed. A cold trickle of sweat ran down my back. I turned around in my seat. "What was all that about?"

She lifted Zach back into his car seat. "What? I just didn't want to get a ticket, that's all." She tucked Zach's arms back into his straps and fastened the buckle across his chest. Her face was flushed, and she didn't meet my gaze.

"And that business about not using your name?" I started up the engine and rejoined the flow of traffic on the freeway.

"I don't know," she said. "I just don't like cops, okay?"

"Yeah, but—"

"Forget it, Theo. It's nothing." She sounded annoyed. "Can we just not talk right now? I want Zach to go to sleep."

I shook my head but said nothing. I turned on the radio, some bland music that I hoped would get me out of singing more Raffi. Angling the rearview mirror, I could see Ronnie stroking Zach's cheek. It looked like he was actually going to doze off. Ronnie's face was tilted toward him, her eyes downcast, her long dark hair falling loose around her shoulders.

She was beautiful, sure. But there was something seriously wrong with this whole picture. I needed to find out exactly what kind of mess I had got myself into.

Chapter Five

I kept driving, careful to stay just under the limit this time, and listened to Ronnie softly coaxing her son to sleep. Finally, there was silence from the backseat. I glanced over my shoulder and saw that Zach was out cold, cheeks flushed and head flopped sideways.

"I shouldn't have had that coffee. I totally have to pee," Ronnie said. "Can we stop somewhere?"

"Yeah." I looked at the gas gauge—half a tank. "Might as well fill up too."

I took the next exit and pulled into a Chevron station half a mile down the road. "Go ahead and use the restroom," I told Ronnie. "I'll get the gas."

"Thanks," she said. "You're a sweetheart."

"No problem," I said. My cheeks were hot, and I felt like scum. She could call me sweetheart all she liked, but I had every intention of searching the car while she was gone. I watched her walk away, then quickly flipped through the plastic folder of papers in the glove box. Everything appeared to be in order. The car was registered to Veronica Gleeson, and her insurance was up-to-date. Not much else in the glove box—a pack of Kleenex, the vehicle owner's manual, a container of green spearmint Tic Tacs.

I popped open the trunk, fully expecting to see something illegal, like Ziploc baggies of white powder, bricks of hash, a stack of marijuana the size of a hay bale. Instead, there was Zach's folded-up stroller, a pile of baby blankets, a box of Huggies, a plastic bag of damp towels and swimsuits, and Ronnie's backpack. Pushing down my feelings of guilt, I unzipped her backpack and flipped the top open. T-shirts, shorts, a soft green cardigan, satiny bras in black and navy and pale pink, red lacy underwear...I closed the bag and zipped it shut again. What the hell was I doing?

I shut the trunk quickly. I had forgotten about the sleeping toddler but was immediately reminded by a loud wail from the backseat.

Crap.

I opened Zach's door. "Hush, hush. Your mom will be right back."

It didn't seem to reassure him much. He stared at me, blue eyes bleary from sleep, and let out another wail.

"Look, I'm going to put gas in the car," I said. "See? I'm putting my debit card in the machine..."

Ronnie appeared at my side. "He woke up, huh?"

"Yeah."

She sighed. "Zachy, you want to go potty?"

He shook his head.

"It's stopping the car," she said. "It always wakes him."

"Mmm." That and me slamming the trunk shut right behind him.

She gestured at the car. "I'm going to try to get him back to sleep. If you need the restroom, you'd better use it now. If we keep driving, hopefully he'll sleep right through to LA."

I went to take a leak. I was starving too. Maybe storming out of the hotel restaurant before eating hadn't been so smart. I bought some pretzels and cashews and a couple of candy bars in the gas-station shop. By the time I got back to the car, Zach's eyes were half-closed again, and Ronnie was singing softly in the backseat beside him.

"Can you drive again?" she whispered.

I nodded. "As long as I don't have to sing any more Raffi." Though I guessed it would serve me right for waking Zach up—and give a whole new meaning to my parents' favorite phrase, *time to face the music*. I tossed the junk food onto the passenger seat, and headed back onto the highway. LA, here we come, I thought. No drugs in the trunk, and we'll be in Hollywood in the morning. I wondered if my parents had found my note yet, or if they were just sitting in the hotel room, watching TV and grumbling about my bad behavior.

I hated the way they didn't trust me, the way they always seemed to assume the worst.

Then again, hadn't I just assumed the worst myself? I hadn't trusted Ronnie. I hadn't even considered that maybe there was some perfectly reasonable explanation for her behavior. Instead, I'd searched her car while she was in the washroom. How was that any better than Mom snooping around my room or Dad looking at my online search history?

God, I was such an asshole. In the rearview mirror I saw that Ronnie's eyes were closed, one wing of silky dark hair partly covering her face. I turned on the radio and scanned through the stations, trying to find something other than country music and eighties rock, but I couldn't shake my sense of foreboding. I needed a straight answer.

"Ronnie," I said softly. There was no answer, but I didn't believe she was really sleeping. I turned the radio off. "Ronnie. I want to know what's going on. That thing with the cop." I looked again at her reflection in the rearview mirror.

She slowly opened her eyes, yawned, blinked sleepily. "Mmm. I must have drifted off."

I gestured to the seat beside me. "How about sitting up here with me? Zach's asleep, and I feel like a cabdriver with you back there."

Ronnie unbuckled her seat belt and climbed forward between the two front seats, her hair so close to my face, I could smell her shampoo.

"Um, I was going to pull over," I told her.

"Don't stop driving—Zach will wake up." She fastened her seat belt.

"That's better," I said. "Hi."

"Hi."

There was a long silence, and I deliberately didn't fill it. Let her feel uncomfortable, I thought. Maybe if she got uncomfortable enough, she'd tell me what was going on.

She cleared her throat. "I guess I acted kind of weird back there. With the cop."

It never failed. Most people just can't handle silence. "Yeah," I said.

Ronnie licked her lips nervously. "This is kind of hard to talk about."

I waited.

She sighed. "Okay. Zach's father... his name is Max. We're not together anymore."

"You're single?" I asked, trying to sound casual. "Uh, that must be hard. With a kid and all."

"Yeah, I'm single." She grinned at me in a way that made it clear she wasn't fooled by my tone. "Too bad I'm your babysitter, huh?"

"Not anymore," I said. My face flooded with heat, and I stared at the road ahead. "Anyway, what's all that got to do with the freak-out over the cop?"

"Max is the kind of guy who likes to be in control. He thinks everything should be a certain way, you know? When we broke up, he pulled some crazy stuff." Ronnie put her hand on my leg. "Theo?"

I looked across at her, my heart racing. Her hand on my leg felt electric. I swallowed hard, trying to sound normal. "Yeah?"

"I'm scared of him." Her eyes met mine, and I could see the fear in her face. "I don't want him to find me."

"You're...are you running away from him?"

"I guess so. Sort of."

"Was he abusive? Did he hit you?" I couldn't imagine anyone hitting her, but I knew it happened all the time. It's crazy how so many men are assholes.

I felt a wave of protectiveness so strong, it caught me off guard. I clenched my fists on the wheel. If he was hurting her…

"I don't really want to get into it," she said, and her voice broke a little.

"Yeah. I mean, of course. I understand," I said.

"I'm scared of him finding me," she said again. "Theo? You'll help me, won't you?"

If Max was abusive, this was a no-brainer. "Of course I will," I told her. "I promise." I put my hand on hers, lacing our fingers together. "When the cop pulled us over…"

She nodded. "I thought maybe he'd run the license plates."

"So what?" I frowned. "It's not Max's car. I mean, you said it wasn't stolen." I didn't think I should mention that I'd seen the registration papers.

She pulled her hand away. "It's not his car," she said quickly. "It's mine."

"So why would it matter?"

"Because he's a cop," she said.

"Duh, I know he was a cop."

Ronnie shook her head impatiently. "No. I mean Max. Zach's dad—he's a cop."

My heart sank. "Please tell me you're kidding."

"I wish."

"There's a crazy abusive cop out there looking for you?" I looked in the rearview mirror. No flashing lights. No sirens.

"He probably has all his buddies looking for me too."

Great. Just great. "I don't suppose he's the jealous type. You know, the kind of dude who might shoot a guy just because he's in the car with his girlfriend?"

"Ex-girlfriend," Ronnie said.

Which didn't exactly answer my question.

Chapter Six

With Zach finally zonked out in the backseat, Ronnie and I took turns driving and sleeping through the night. By the time we arrived on the outskirts of LA, the sun was coming up. The horizon was streaked with vivid orange, and the darker sky above looked almost purple.

I pulled the car over to the side of the road, since I had no idea where in the city Ronnie's friend lived. "Wake up, Ronnie," I whispered. "We're here."

Ronnie yawned and stretched. "Awesome."

I pointed out the window. "That's some sunrise, huh?"

"It's the pollution," she said sleepily. "Dirty cities have the best sunrises."

We switched positions, Ronnie taking the wheel. Zach, thankfully, stirred only briefly before sticking his thumb back into his mouth and slipping back to sleep. As Ronnie drove, I watched the lines of traffic snaking their way into the city and the skyscrapers of downtown beginning to push up along the horizon in a jagged concrete line.

I wondered what Darrell would say when my parents called him. Probably he'd shake his head disapprovingly and mutter something lame about "kids these days." It was kind of hard to believe that Darrell had ever been a teenager himself.

According to my parents, he'd always been perfect. *Darrell always did so well in math, Theo. I don't remember Darrell's friends ever getting into the kind of trouble your friends seem to find themselves in. Darrell never spoke to your mother in that tone, young man.*

I shook my head to clear the thoughts. I had enough to worry about right now, what with Ronnie's gun-toting ex on our heels. "Where's your friend live?" I asked.

She tossed me a printout of a Google map. "Can you navigate? I've never actually been here."

"Yeah." I studied the page for a minute. "Stay on this highway. I'll tell you when we're near the exit." I traced the route with my finger and hoped I wouldn't get us too lost. Apparently Ronnie's friend lived on Harrison Street, which seemed like a good omen. The name made me think of Harrison Ford, which made me think of Han Solo. "So this friend. You said she works in the movie industry?"

"I think so. I mean, that's why she moved here."

"She's from Portland?"

Ronnie nodded. "We were in high school together. She posted something on Facebook awhile back about getting a part in a movie."

"Like, acting? Cool."

"Yeah." She gave me a sideways look. "Joelle's gorgeous."

Which for some stupid reason made me blush.

It took us awhile to find Joelle's apartment, and the closer we got, the more my heart sank. The neighborhood looked like the kind guidebooks advise you not to walk through after dark: empty storefronts, overflowing dumpsters, graffiti and a distinct lack of trees and grass.

"This is it," Ronnie said, parking the car. "She said the entrance is around the back. It's a basement suite."

"Right," I said. "Of course it is."

She gave me a sharp look but said nothing as she unbuckled Zach and lifted him onto her hip. I grabbed my bag from the backseat and her backpack from the trunk, and followed her around the side of the building to the back door.

Ronnie knocked loudly. "I hope she's home. My credit card's almost maxed out."

"Isn't she expecting you?"

"Um, sort of. I mean, not today, exactly. But she's always saying on Facebook that I should come visit LA."

My heart sank even further. I wasn't sure that qualified as an invitation. "What if she's not here? I mean, I've got about four hundred bucks in the bank. But that's not going to last long if we have to get a hotel room."

She raised one eyebrow, and I remembered how she had put her hand on my thigh when she was telling me about Max. I felt my face getting hot. "Not that, you know, I'm saying we would get a hotel room, necessarily. I mean, not together. But—"

To my relief, the door opened before I could make matters worse.

"Ronnie? Ronnie Gleeson? Oh my god!" A tall, very blond girl stood in front of us. From the tousled hair and the fact that she was wearing nothing but a pink T-shirt, I gathered we had woken her up. "What are you doing here?"

"Joelle!" Ronnie gave her a one-armed hug. "This is my baby, Zach! Isn't he gorgeous?"

"He's a doll," Joelle said. She had long legs, smooth and tanned, and the

T-shirt she was wearing didn't cover much at all. I tried not to stare.

"We just drove all night," Ronnie said. She looked at me, laughed and turned back to Joelle. "I can't believe we're here."

"Me neither." Joelle looked at me. "Hi. I'm Joelle."

"Sorry, sorry." Ronnie shook her head. "I'm a bit out of it. This is my buddy, Theo." She giggled. "Get this, Jo—I used to babysit him."

I really wished she hadn't just said that. "It was a long time ago," I told Joelle.

She looked me up and down, not even trying to hide that she was totally checking me out. Then she turned to Ronnie and raised one eyebrow. "I guess so," she said, grinning. "Come on in, you guys. I'll make coffee."

Joelle's apartment was a dive. I'm no neat freak, as my mom often points out, but it's one thing to leave clothes lying around and another thing altogether to let dirty dishes and overflowing ashtrays and beer and wine bottles take over every horizontal surface.

I moved an empty pizza box off a chair, and Ronnie deposited her still-sleeping toddler, who promptly woke up and started to cry.

I'd never met a kid who cried so much, but maybe toddlers always cried when they woke up. I was no expert.

Ronnie pulled a box of Ritz crackers from her bag, which seemed to cheer Zach up, and Joelle put on a pot of coffee. She eyed my duffel bag and Ronnie's backpack. "So, are you guys just passing through?"

Ronnie perched on the arm of Zach's chair. "Actually, we were wondering if we could crash with you for a few days."

Joelle rummaged around in a cupboard and found a couple of mugs.

"Um, yeah, sure. If you don't mind the couch or the floor. I only have one bedroom."

"That's fine," Ronnie said. "We really appreciate you letting us stay."

I looked around. It seemed to me we'd have to do a fair bit of work to find the couch and the floor, and the thought of sleeping on either of them was less than appealing. "What about Zach?" I said.

"He can sleep in his stroller," Ronnie said. She had dark circles under her eyes, and her voice sounded strained. "He'll be fine."

I nodded.

Zach crumbled a Ritz cracker in his fist. "Dada," he said. "Dada."

"Not now, Zach." Ronnie looked at me. "I don't have the energy to deal with him sometimes, you know?"

This apartment was enough to suck the last dregs of strength from anyone.

"Come on," I said. "Let's go do something. We're in LA!" I bent down to ruffle Zach's dark hair. "Universal Studios? What do you say?"

"Theo!" Ronnie laughed. "You have any idea what that costs?"

I shrugged. "Not a clue, actually. But we might as well get out for the day."

"Yeah," Joelle said. "I have to work tonight, so I need to sleep this morning."

"Ronnie said you had a job in the movie business."

"Uh, yeah. Well, I acted in a couple of films. But tonight I'm just waitressing." She yawned widely. "I'll give you my spare key, okay? But if you could stay out until, like, three or four, that'd be cool."

"Sure," I said. "I mean, thanks. For letting us crash here."

"Ronnie and me, we go way back," Joelle said.

Chapter Seven

It turned out that Ronnie was right. Getting the three of us into Universal Studios would have cost almost two hundred bucks. Which was half the money in my bank account.

"Zach's probably too young for the rides anyway," Ronnie said. "Joelle said we should check out CityWalk. At least it's free."

I'd never heard of CityWalk. It turned out to be several blocks of shops and restaurants and movie theaters, starting right outside the entrance to Universal Studios. Brightly colored signs were everywhere. A three-story-high guitar hung in front of a Hard Rock Café, and a massive King Kong leaned over the street, looking ready to grab passersby.

Ronnie laughed and handed me her phone. "Take my picture, Theo." She posed in front of the gorilla's enormous hand, and I backed up, angling the camera so that it looked as though she was just about to be snatched up like the chick in the *King Kong* movie.

Zach fussed in his stroller, squirming and whimpering. "You want to get out, little buddy?" I asked him. "Want to run around a bit?" I fumbled with the straps, which seemed remarkably complicated, until Ronnie came and took over. She freed Zach with a couple of quick clicks, and he clambered down.

"Want to see?" I asked, showing her the photo on her phone.

"Hold it still." She put her hand over mine, shading the screen from the sun. Her fingers were soft and cool against my own. "Oh, that's awesome! It looks totally real. I'm putting this one on Facebook." Then she frowned and pulled her hand away. "Or not, I guess."

"What?" I handed her the phone. "Oh, right. I guess that'd kind of let everyone know where you are. But your ex doesn't still have access to your Facebook, does he?"

"Of course not." She watched Zach, who was running about in wildly unpredictable zigzags and generally getting in the way of everyone walking past. "We have a lot of the same friends though."

"Your friends would tell him where you are?" I shook my head. "That's awful, Ronnie. Do they know what happened? I mean, how he treated you?"

She shrugged. "I don't want to talk about it." She slipped her cell phone back into her purse. "I need a coffee. Can you watch Zach for a minute?"

"Uh, sure. Yeah." I wished she wouldn't keep shutting me out.

"You want anything?"

I shook my head. "I'm good."

Ronnie disappeared into a Starbucks, and I kept both my eyes on Zach, which was a challenge. He moved fast. When he ran past me, I reached out and tapped his shoulder. "Hey, buddy. Where are you off to?"

He gave me a smile, showing two rows of tiny pearl-white teeth. "Theo," he said.

"Hey, buddy. You said my name!" I grinned at him. He was pretty cute when he wasn't crying. "So what do you think, Zach? Does a guy like me have a chance with someone as gorgeous as your mom?" I sounded like Han Solo. *You think a guy like me and a princess like her...*

"Raisins," Zach said.

I sighed, looked under the stroller and came up empty-handed. "I don't know, kiddo. It doesn't look too good for either of us."

Finally Ronnie returned, a coffee in one hand and a paper bag in the other. "Zach, I got you a muffin." She broke off a piece and handed it to him. "So, guess what, Theo? They're hiring at the Starbucks."

I frowned. "You're looking for a job?"

"I can't," she said. "I have Zach. But I thought you might be."

"At Starbucks?" I shook my head. "Wasn't exactly what I had in mind."

"Right by Universal Studios though. You might meet all kinds of movie people."

"All kinds of tourists, more like." I shook my head. "I don't know, Ronnie. I didn't get the impression Joelle was up for having us stay long term." I hadn't thought very far ahead—actually, I hadn't *thought*, period—but I probably had to go home at some point.

A road trip was one thing. A permanent move to LA was something else altogether.

Ronnie's forehead crinkled above her sunglasses. "Her place is pretty small."

"It's a disaster zone," I said bluntly.

"Yeah." She bit her bottom lip. "I know. But I'm broke, so…"

"So you want me to get a job?" I pushed back a wave of anger. "Is that why you brought me along?"

"No! I mean, I hadn't really thought everything through."

"No kidding," I said. My voice came out harsher than I'd intended. "You just took off to LA with no money at all. Brilliant plan, Ronnie."

"You didn't have to come," she flashed back. "Anyway, it's not like you have money either."

"Yeah, but that's different. I don't have a kid to look after." I looked down at Zach, who was solemnly chewing his muffin and looking up at us. "You can't just couch-surf around Hollywood with a baby."

"I'm not going to," she said. "I just haven't figured out all the details yet."

It was weird—she was five years older than me, and no one had ever accused me of being unusually mature, but right now I felt like I was the older one. "You said Joelle had connections in the movie industry," I reminded her.

"You said she'd be able to get me a job."

"Yeah. I know." She took her sunglasses off, and her eyes were shining with tears. "I'm sorry. I'm messed up, Theo. All this stuff with Zach's dad…"

I put an arm around her awkwardly. To my surprise, she leaned her head against my shoulder. I wished I could fix things for her. "Ronnie. It'll be okay," I whispered. I wasn't sure it would be, not really, but I had to say something.

"I'm just tired," she said. "Sorry. I don't usually lose it like this."

Her hair tickled my face, and she smelled like vanilla. "It's okay," I said.

She lifted her head and looked up at me. "I shouldn't have pulled you into my stupid, messy life."

"Don't say that." My anger had completely dissolved. "I'm glad I ran into you. And it'll all work out. Who knows, maybe I'll be the next Walt Disney."

She managed a laugh. "It's funny that you're still into animation. Remember how you used to love comic books? Superheroes and all that stuff?"

"Uh-huh."

"You even had those cute—"

"Please don't mention the R2-D2 pajamas," I said.

She laughed, and this time it sounded genuine. "You were adorable."

"I was a geek," I admitted.

"An adorable geek." She was quiet for a moment. "Look, whatever you decide to do, it's cool. I mean, really. My messy life is not your problem."

"Yes, it is," I said. "I mean, you're my friend. I care about what happens to you, Ronnie." It was true—but at the same time, I was wondering how exactly I'd got myself into this situation. Just yesterday—not even twenty-four hours ago—I was a high school kid on vacation with my folks, with nothing more to worry about than nagging parents and unfinished homework. I felt like I'd jumped to lightspeed and ended up in some alternate universe in which I seemed to be responsible for, well, everything. What the hell had I been thinking? I wished there was an easy way out...but I couldn't see one.

"I don't know what I'm going to do," I said at last. "I guess I'll talk to Joelle later, see if she has any job leads. And I should call my folks. They'll be at Darrell's place by this afternoon. I should let them know where I am."

I wasn't looking forward to that phone call at all.

Chapter Eight

By the time we got back to her apartment, Joelle was up and showered, dressed in a very short black dress and making dinner. "It's just spaghetti," she said. "Cooking's not really my thing."

"Spaghetti's great," Ronnie said. "It's, like, one of the three things Zach eats. Seriously. Raisins, Ritz crackers and spaghetti."

"Don't you worry about him getting sick?" Joelle said. "I mean, if he's not eating properly?"

"He's fine," Ronnie said. "Aren't you, Zach? Want some spaghetti, sweetie?" She beckoned to him. "Joelle's making spaghetti."

"Is he chewing something?" I asked. "What's he got?"

Ronnie grabbed him. "Open up, Zach. What is it? Spit it out." She fished around in his mouth and scooped something out. "Oh, gross, Zachy! That's a cigarette butt."

"That's four things he eats then," I said.

Ronnie scowled at me. "Not funny, Theo." She put Zach back down, a little harder than necessary. "Bad, Zach! Dirty."

Zach started to cry, and Ronnie swore under her breath. "I need a shower. Can you just watch him for a few minutes?"

"Sure, yeah." I picked Zach up and bounced him up and down, wondering what the hell to do. Ronnie and I were both broke, but we couldn't stay here. This apartment was way too small, and when I looked around with Zach in mind, it seemed like there was dangerous stuff everywhere. An open pair of scissors on a coffee table, a bottle of laundry detergent on the floor, a bottle of prescription meds on the arm of the couch, half-empty beer bottles on the window ledge...

Cigarette butts were the least of the problems.

"Hey, Joelle?" I cleared my throat and spoke over Zach's sobs. "Ronnie mentioned that you might have some connections in the movie industry?"

She laughed. "Did she?"

"Yeah. The thing is, I've always been kind of interested in getting into making movies. That was part of the reason I wanted to come here, actually."

She handed me a jar of spaghetti sauce. "Can you open this for me?"

I put Zach, who was still crying, down on the floor, twisted the lid off and handed it back to her. "I mean, animation is what I'm really into, but anything would be great, just to get a foot in the door, you know?"

She put the jar down and turned to look at me. "Ronnie didn't tell you what kind of movies I was in, did she?"

"No."

"Right." She sighed. "Theo, you're a sweet guy. And you're a good-looking kid...but you don't want to take advantage of any connections I have, okay?"

"What do you mean?"

"Trust me," she said.

It took me a few seconds, and then I felt my cheeks heating up. "Do you mean...the movies you acted in...

were they...?" I didn't want to say "porn," but I couldn't think of a more appropriate word.

"Adult movies," she said. "Skin flicks. Not hard-core, but you know, X-rated."

"Right." I didn't know where to look.

She laughed. "Awww. You're such an innocent."

If my face hadn't been bright red a minute ago, it certainly was now. I picked Zach back up and bounced him up and down a few times just to give myself an excuse not to look at Joelle. His sobs subsided, and he put his head down on my shoulder, like he was sleepy. "Gotcha," I said. "Well, cool."

"This city is a crazy place, Theo. Everyone just sees the bright lights and the glamor, but underneath all that, there's a lot of broken hearts. People come here with big dreams..."

She trailed off and shrugged. "It wasn't that bad, but I kind of wish I hadn't done it, you know?"

I nodded, feeling like I knew absolutely nothing about anything. "Um, yeah."

"You planning on sticking around LA?"

"I don't know." Zach tugged on the collar of my T-shirt. I put him down on the kitchen floor and found him a set of measuring spoons to play with. "Ronnie seems like she needs a bit of help, you know?"

Joelle shook her head. "What else is new?"

"What do you mean?"

She shrugged. "I love that girl, but she just goes from crisis to crisis, doesn't she?"

"Does she?" I grabbed the strap of Zach's overalls as he started to scoot off into the living room, presumably to chow down on some more cigarette butts. "Can't his dad help out at all? I mean, she should at least get child support, right?"

Joelle raised her hands. "I'm staying out of it."

"But if he's a cop, he must earn a decent salary. Even if he's a jerk, he's got to help out financially."

She laughed. "A cop? Where'd you get that idea? Max isn't a cop—he's a teacher. High school, I think."

I stared at her. "What?"

"He wasn't *her* teacher, don't worry. Though he *is* too old for her. Like, almost ten years older than she is." She made a face. "When they got together, she was nineteen and he was twenty-eight, which is kind of pervy, if you ask me. Not that Max was pervy. He was a great guy. Gentle, you know?"

I shook my head. "Ronnie said he was a cop."

Joelle pulled the saucepan off the burner. "I have to get going, okay? The spaghetti sauce is there, dishes in the cupboard." She ruffled Zach's hair. "See you tomorrow, little guy."

"Are you sure he's not a cop?"

"Yeah, I'm sure." She slipped one foot into a strappy shoe with an ultra-high heel. "Where the hell's my other shoe? God, this place is a mess...Oh, there it is. Bye, Theo."

"Bye." I waved and watched her walk out the door. Then I caught a whiff of something that definitely wasn't dinner. "Zach? Did you...? Ugh. You did, didn't you?" I picked him up and held him well out in front of me. "Uh, Ronnie? Where are you? I kind of need you out here."

"Coming, coming!" Ronnie stepped out of the bathroom, wrapped in a pink towel, her hair still dripping.

"I think he just took a dump."

She sighed. "Can't you just change his diaper? There should be a couple of clean ones in the blue bag."

I stood there, frozen, my arms still held stiffly out, zombie style, with Zach starting to squirm between them.

"Oh my god, Theo, it's just poo." Apparently she noticed my expression, because she broke off. "Fine. I'll do it." She took him from me, forehead creased in annoyance. "You'd think it was nuclear waste from the look on your face."

"Sorry," I said sheepishly. "I don't have much experience with, you know, diapers."

She snorted. "Can you at least grab me my bag?"

"Sure," I said, relieved. "And dinner's ready when you are."

Chapter Nine

Half an hour later, the three of us were sitting at the tiny kitchen table. Ronnie had blow-dried her hair and piled it on top of her head in some kind of fancy-looking twist. She was wearing tight jeans and a strapless red top, and she looked stunning. I had poured glasses of wine from a bottle on the counter and dished up plates of spaghetti for everyone. We looked like a regular family, except that Zach was falling asleep and Ronnie was tense, drinking the wine like it was apple juice and biting my head off every time I tried to talk to her.

I got the meal off to a bad start by asking her about Max. "Joelle said he's a teacher," I began.

"Yeah, he is. So?"

"You told me he was a cop."

She froze for a split second, her eyes wide. Somehow she managed to look both guilty and innocent—like a puppy that just got caught chewing a sneaker. "I did?"

"Yeah. You did. When we got pulled over, remember?" My heart was beating faster than usual. Had she actually *lied* to me?

"Oh yeah." She didn't even blush. "I just thought he might have cops looking for me, that's all."

It seemed like a weird thing to lie about. "So why not just say that?"

"I don't know, Theo. Jeez. I was just freaked out. Like I said, I don't want him to find me."

Joelle had said he was a nice guy. This didn't fit with my theory that he was a crazy stalker, but then again, you never really knew anything about a relationship from the outside. "Why are you scared of him?" I asked.

She scowled at me and twirled spaghetti around her fork. "Can we talk about something else, please?"

"Right." I took a sip of the wine and made a face. It tasted like vinegar. "I was thinking, you should get child support, right? I mean, he's still responsible—"

She cut me off. "I said drop it, Theo."

I couldn't though. "It's just…neither of us has much money. How are you going to manage? I mean, you can't really work with Zach to look after, and this place—well, staying here isn't really a long-term solution, is it?"

Ronnie put her fork down. She sat there, not moving, and just stared at me for a long moment. Then she stood, picked up Zach and carried him into the living room.

I followed her. "Ronnie. Come on. I'm sorry. Don't be mad. I just think we have to deal with this. You can't keep running away from problems, you know? We have to figure out what to do."

She lowered Zach into his stroller, reclined the seat and snapped the seat belt closed. "I'm going out," she said. "I need a break, okay?"

"What?" She was making me crazy. "No, Ronnie, it's not okay. We have to talk."

"Not now."

"Yes, now. Why won't you just tell me what's going on?" I tried to catch her eye, but she wouldn't look at me.

I reached out and touched her bare shoulder. Her skin was silk-smooth and warm. "I'm on your side here. I want to help. You know that."

"Then watch Zach for me for a bit, would you? I just need to get out on my own for a couple hours." She pulled a blanket over Zach's lap. "He'll be fine. He probably won't even wake up until the morning."

"I guess, but..."

"Thanks, Theo." She turned and kissed me, right on the lips. Her mouth tasted like wine and strawberry lip gloss. It could have been just a casual, friendly kiss—except that it wasn't. Ronnie pulled back, staring at me. Her eyes were wide and dark, the pupils dilated and swallowing up the blue.

I felt like I'd just been hit by lightning. "Um, wow. I wasn't expecting that."

"Sorry. I, uh..." Ronnie's cheeks were flushed.

"Shhh." I slid my hand under her hair, into that soft, warm hidden place on the back of the neck, and I tilted her face up toward mine. Her lips parted and my mouth was on hers, my fingers tangling in her hair, and I was kissing her with an intensity that took my breath away. Ronnie's hands were gripping my shoulders, her body pressed against mine. My fingers traced the soft skin of her back between the low-rise jeans and the tank top. I couldn't believe this was happening. I couldn't believe I was kissing Ronnie Gleeson.

And then she broke away. "Wow. Okay. Um, I'll see you later, Theo." She grabbed her purse from the couch. "Bye."

"Ronnie..." But she was already out the front door. I watched her walk away and then collapsed into the closest chair.

She was infuriating. I remembered one of my favorite Han Solo lines—

Wonderful girl. Either I'm going to kill her or I'm beginning to like her. I took a deep breath and tried to calm down. I was all jangled heartbeat and electric nerve endings. And underneath that, I was dead tired. I watched Zach sleeping in his stroller for a minute, his lashes dark against his cheeks, his little mouth slightly open.

I knew I had to call my parents. I'd been putting it off all day, but it wasn't fair to leave them worrying. I finally found Joelle's phone, half-buried in a pile of dirty laundry, and collect-called my brother's place.

"Darrell?"

"Theo!" He dropped his voice a notch. "Mom and Dad are not happy campers, pal. You are in deep, deep doo-doo."

Doo-doo? I rolled my eyes. "Right, yeah. I figured they'd be pissed."

"What were you thinking? Mom said you took off with Ronnie Gleeson.

She's Tom Gleeson's little sister, isn't she? I went to school with him."

"Yeah, I guess." I'd forgotten that she even had a brother. "She's twenty-two now though. She has a kid."

"I heard." He lowered his voice even further, and I wondered where Mom and Dad were. "Did you guys hook up?"

Hook up. It sounded funny, coming from Darrell. "No," I said. "Well, not really."

He laughed. "You did, didn't you?"

"It's not like that." I hesitated.

"Why'd you take off so fast?"

"I don't know. Mom and Dad were on my case about drugs like you wouldn't believe. Searching my room, sniffing my breath, giving me lecture after lecture. I'd had enough, I guess."

"They told me about your buddy Koli." He cleared his throat. "So, you weren't involved?"

"No. God, don't you start."

"Don't panic. I believe you."

"Good."

There was a pause, then Darrell said, "They just worry, you know. It was the same for me. Worse, I bet."

I snorted. "Get serious. They're always going on about how you never caused them this kind of stress, you never had an attitude like mine, you never—"

He cut me off. "Then they'd better get checked out for early-onset Alzheimer's, pal. I know you were just a kid when I moved out, but that sure isn't how I remember it."

"Come on. You were a straight A student, valedictorian, early college entrance, all that stuff. I hear about it all the time."

"Yeah." He gave a short laugh. "I worked my tail off trying to make them happy, and they were convinced that disaster was just around the corner the whole time. Drinking and driving—that was their big obsession with me. It's how they are, Theo."

"Seriously?" I wasn't sure I believed him.

"For what it's worth, I told them to lighten up on you."

"Yeah?"

"Yeah." He was quiet for a moment. "Look, I'm not saying you did the right thing, taking off like this. I mean, it was pretty inconsiderate. But it's not really like you to do something like that. Maybe you needed to, you know, break away a little."

"Maybe," I said.

"Anyway"—Darrell suddenly sounded businesslike—"I suppose you want to talk to our parents. Dad just walked in. I'll put him on."

"Okay. Thanks, Darrell."

My dad's voice came on the line. "Theo? Where are you?"

"Los Angeles."

"With Ronnie Gleeson." He sounded furious. "We used to pay her to babysit you, you know. And now she pulls a stunt like this. Unbelievable."

"It's not her fault," I said. "I told her I had your permission. I'm sorry though. I didn't mean to make you guys worry. I just, I didn't really think it through."

"Well, that much is clear."

I felt a wave of the same old frustration. Why couldn't he ever meet me halfway? "Look," I said. "I'm tired of you guys not trusting me."

"This behavior hardly seems likely to help with that."

"I know, I know. I already said sorry." I watched Zach sleeping and tried to calm down. "It's the drug thing. I don't deal drugs. I don't even use drugs."

"Koli—"

"Is my best friend. Does he have a problem? Yes, okay, he does. But I'm not going to just turn my back on him, Dad."

He didn't say anything.

"Dad?"

"Yeah, all right, Theo. I heard you." He muttered something I couldn't hear, and I could make out my mother's voice in the background. Then Dad spoke again. "We want you to take a bus to Santa Rosa tonight, Theo. I'll check the schedule right now."

"I can't," I said. "Ronnie's out and I'm watching her son."

"You're babysitting?"

"I guess you could call it that."

Dad said something that sounded a lot like "harrumph." I guess it was sort of funny, in a way—me babysitting my babysitter's kid.

"In the morning then," he said.

I hesitated. I didn't want to leave Ronnie, but I had a life back home.

School, family, friends. Ronnie's promises about connections in the movie industry hadn't exactly led anywhere. And Ronnie herself—well, she might need help, but she wouldn't even talk to me about her problems.

I could still feel her kiss burning on my lips. That kiss might have kept me here, if I hadn't suspected that she'd just done it to get me to say I'd look after Zach.

You can't keep running away from your problems, I'd told her. Maybe I should take my own advice. "Okay," I said at last. "In the morning."

I hung up, watched TV for a couple of hours and curled up in the chair to sleep. When I woke up, pale morning light was creeping through the high windows, and Zach was starting to stir and whimper in his stroller.

And Ronnie was nowhere to be seen.

Chapter Ten

I lifted Zach out of his stroller. "Shhh, shhh," I whispered. "We don't want to wake Joelle."

"Dada," Zach said, snuffling a bit. "Dada."

"Um, nope, just me. Not your Dada," I said. Then I realized he was pushing me away and looking around the room. "Your dad's not here, Zach." And neither

is your mom, I thought, but I didn't say
it out loud. Instead I tiptoed across the
living room, shushing Zach, and pushed
open the door to Joelle's bedroom.

No one there. Just a heap of blue
sheets on the bed and a mess of clothes
everywhere.

So it was just me and Zach. What
the hell was up with that? But there was
no time to think about it, because Zach
was fussing and squirming to be put
down. "I guess you need some breakfast," I said to him. "And I need some
coffee. Very. Strong. Coffee. Lots of it.
Come on, buddy."

I sat Zach down on the kitchen
counter and opened a few cupboards.
"Hey look, buddy—instant coffee.
And Rice Krispies! You like those?"

He didn't look thrilled.

"Or look—there's milk in the
fridge. You want some milk?" I poured
him a glass and switched on the kettle.

Ronnie must be out with Joelle some-where, but it was pretty uncool of her. Surely she knew her kid would wake up and want her. I watched Zach drink his milk and pushed back my anger. She was totally taking advantage of me, but worse than that was how unfair she was being to Zach. The poor kid barely knew me.

I wiped the milk that was dribbling down his chin. "How about some music, buddy? Let's see if Joelle's got any good tunes." A few minutes later, Zach was happily sitting and listening to some techno-pop and pulling all the Kleenex out of a box he'd found on the living-room floor. He looked a little bulky around the bum, and I had a feeling he needed a diaper change.

To my relief, the front door opened. I jumped to my feet. "Hey! I'm so glad you're back. I was worried that some-thing had happened."

Joelle stepped inside and closed the door behind her. "I worked until two and then some of the girls invited me out with them." She saw the look on my face. "What's wrong? Where's Ronnie?"

"She's not with you?" My heart sank. Actually, *sank* is too gentle a word. My heart plummeted like an elevator with a snapped cable.

"No. I haven't seen her since I left for work last night."

I flopped into the armchair and rubbed my hands over my face, suddenly feeling completely exhausted. "I have no clue where she is, Joelle. She took off last night. Said she needed a break for a couple of hours."

"She left you with him?" Joelle nodded at Zach, who was sitting in the middle of a mountain of snow-white Kleenex.

"I guess so. Yeah."

"That sucks." Her forehead was furrowed. "She'll probably be back soon though." She didn't sound entirely convinced.

"What is it?" I said.

She shook her head. "Ronnie likes to party. Sometimes she drinks too much, you know?"

I shrugged. Most people did, it seemed to me. My parents sure did. Which reminded me…"Yeah. I'm supposed to be catching a bus this morning." I'd have to call my folks if I didn't, and they were not going to be impressed.

"I can't take him," Joelle said. "I gotta sleep. I work again tonight."

I studied Zach. He'd been wearing that diaper all night, and it had to be soaked by now. Ronnie's blue bag was on the floor, and I opened it up. A hoodie, Ritz crackers, a bag of raisins, a magazine…

and not much else. The rest of her stuff was in the car, which she had taken with her last night. "Joelle? I don't suppose you have any diapers around."

Joelle laughed. "Uh, no. Sorry, Theo. There's a Walmart close though." She pointed. "Out to the main drag, left at the lights, walk along a couple of blocks. You can't miss it."

"Thanks." Should I ask her to watch Zach for me while I got diapers? Maybe I could even persuade her to do the diaper change…

She hid a yawn behind her hand. "Sorry, Theo. I have to hit the sack."

"Right." I sighed and picked Zach up. "Come on, kiddo. We have a mission." I loaded Zach into his stroller, buckled him in and headed out. It was already hot, and the air felt heavy and damp. By the time we got to the Walmart, I was sweating. I pushed the stroller through the automatic doors and into a wall of frosty air conditioning.

The store was pretty empty. We cruised down the first aisle, and Zach started to squirm and struggle against his stroller straps. "You need to walk a bit, buddy?" I unbuckled him. "Come on. You can help me find the diapers, okay?"

"Diapers," Zach said, pointing.

We were standing by a whole wall of them. "Duh. Thanks, kiddo." I remembered that there had been a box of Huggies in the car, but apparently these things came in various sizes. Okay, not newborn, obviously, but beyond that there still seemed to be a lot of choices. What did Zach weigh? Twenty pounds? Thirty? I figured it was better to get diapers too big than too small, and since the toddler pictured on the box for thirty-pound kids looked about Zach's age, I reached to grab it.

Then I realized those ones were for girls. The pink packaging should have been the clue, I guess, but who knew they made diapers differently for boys and girls? And where were the thirty-pound-boy diapers?

"You want Donald Duck or Lightning McQueen on your diapers?" I asked, looking down. But Zach wasn't there anymore.

"Zach!" I looked up and down the aisle and didn't see him. *Crap. Crap, crap, crap.* "Zach!" I yelled again.

No answer. He had completely disappeared. I shouldn't have let him out of the stroller. I shouldn't have let him out of the house. I shouldn't have taken my eyes off him for a single goddamn second. Which way had he gone? I took a few steps to the end of the aisle and glanced to the right and then to the left.

No sign of him.

Where the hell was he? I ran past the diapers, past the baby food, past the rattles and toys. "Zach! Come here, Zachy!"

God, what if he was really lost? Or worse? What if he'd been snatched by some pervert, or wandered out the doors into traffic, or...

And there, just around the corner, sitting on a bright blue-and-white display potty, was Zach. I felt an overwhelming wave of relief that made my legs feel weak. He was fine. I hadn't lost him after all. And then I realized that his tiny cargo shorts and pull-up diaper were down around his ankles.

"No, no, Zach! You can't..." I stepped toward him and realized from the look of concentration on his face that I might be too late. A second later, the potty began playing an upbeat musical number, and a strong smell confirmed my fears. Little Zachy had just made a doo-doo.

"Zach go potty," he informed me. The kid had the nerve to sound pleased about it.

"Great," I said. "That's just great. I'm sure your mama will be proud."

"Mama," he said. His bottom lip quivered. "Dada. Mama."

I blew out a breath. I shouldn't have mentioned that word. "You'll see her soon," I said, and I hoped to God it was true. But right now I had a more immediate problem to deal with. I looked up and down the aisle. No one was paying any attention to us. I lifted Zach up, pulled up his wet diaper and pants, and closed the potty lid. "Okay, kiddo. Time for us to get away from the scene of the crime."

I tucked Zach back into his stroller, paid for a box of Donald Duck Pull-Ups and fled, pushing the stroller out the door without a backward glance.

At least that was one nasty diaper change I wouldn't have to deal with.

I was half expecting Ronnie to be sitting in the living room when I got back, but there was still no sign of her. I stripped off Zach's wet diaper and helped him into a clean, dry one, feeding his chubby legs through the elastic leg holes. He should have clean pants too, but his clothes were all in the car. I spotted Ronnie's blue bag on the floor and opened it up again. "Zach, how about some raisins?"

He beamed at me. "Raisins."

"Great." I pulled out a half-full jumbo bag—and underneath it was Ronnie's cell phone. I hadn't even known she had one, or I'd have been trying to call her. I pulled it out of the bag and turned it on. The ringer was off, but she had a ton of text messages.

I hesitated but only for a second. Password? How about *Zach*?

Bingo.

I handed Zach the raisins and scrolled through the messages. There were about thirty, and it didn't look like she'd replied to any of them. I started at the beginning, three nights earlier.

What's up? You're late.

Are you on your way?

Where are you, Ronnie? Call me.

Hey, are you okay? I thought we said five o'clock.

Ronnie, we're all freaking out a little. It's Zach's bedtime. Where the hell are you?

I'm calling the police if I don't hear from you by morning.

And the next day.

Ronnie, I don't want to get the cops involved. Call me. We'll figure this out.

Damn it Ronnie. This is messed up. At least let me know you're both okay.

Trying again. Call me.

Drove over to your house. Again. Where the hell are you?

Think about Zach. This isn't fair to him or me.

Ronnie, if you don't call me I'm going to call the cops. Seriously.

And the day after that.

Called the cops. You know this is kidnapping, right?

I felt a clutch of shock deep in my chest, like someone had just grabbed my heart and squeezed it, hard. *Cops? Kidnapping?* I stared at the words on the screen until they began blurring in their little green text boxes. My legs were wobbly. I sank into the chair and Zach looked solemnly up at me, chewing. *Kidnapped.* The phone was slippery in my hand.

There were more texts—*Just come home. We'll figure it out. Ronnie, the longer you stay away the worse it looks.*

What the hell are you planning, Ronnie? You can't just disappear—but I'd read enough.

I started typing: *I'm a friend of Ronnie's. What's going on?*

Seconds later, the phone vibrated in my hand. I answered quickly. "Hello?"

"Hi." A man's voice. "Who is this?"

"Uh, my name's Theo. I'm a friend of Ronnie's."

"Is she there? Put her on."

"No. She's not. Is this Max?" I tried to remember exactly what she had told me about him.

"Yeah. Where is she? Does she have Zach?" His voice was strained. "Are they okay?"

"They're fine," I said. "Zach's right here, actually."

"Let me talk to him."

"Uh, okay." I held the phone by Zach's ear and waited.

I could hear Max's voice. "Zach, baby!"

Zach's eyes widened, and he dropped the bag of raisins. "Dada?"

"Yes, it's Dada. I miss you, Zachy."

"Dada, dada, dada." Zach pulled his head back and studied the phone for a moment, as if he might be able to see his father in it. I tried to put it back to his ear.

"Zach, you're going to come home now, okay? Dada's going to come get you. I'll see you soon."

"Home. Zach home dada." Zach's face crumpled, and he looked like he was about to cry.

"Soon, Zach, okay? I promise."

I handed Zach the raisins again, hoping to distract him, and spoke into the phone. "Hi. It's me again."

"Who did you say you were? And where the hell is Ronnie?" he said.

"My name's Theo," I said again. "I'm a friend of Ronnie's."

"Right. Why do you have Zach? And where is she?"

"She went out. She asked me to watch him for a few hours."

"Where are you? I'll come get Zach right now."

I hesitated. Ronnie had said she was scared of Max finding her, and I'd assumed he was abusive. "Are you a cop?" I asked.

He snorted. "I'm a teacher. But I called the cops, if that's what you mean. I didn't want to, but she wouldn't return my calls or my texts. No one knew where she'd gone. Which, frankly, I wouldn't care about at this point. But she took Zach."

I was slowly putting the puzzle pieces together. It wasn't the car that she'd stolen.

It was the kid.

Chapter Eleven

I picked Zach up and sank back down onto the chair with him on my lap. I took a deep breath and exhaled slowly. Freaking out wasn't going to help. Besides, it wasn't really stealing if it was your own kid, was it? And no matter what she'd done, Ronnie was Zach's mother. "You have shared custody?" I said. "And she took off?"

"I have sole custody," he said grimly. "Ronnie has a visit with Zach every Saturday. She's supposed to have him back here by five, but this week she never showed up. I've been frantic. Where the hell are you?"

"Yeah. Uh, I just found her phone and saw all your texts." How was I supposed to know if he was telling the truth? Sure, Ronnie had lied about some stuff, but that didn't mean I could trust Max.

"Is she there, really? I mean, does she just not want to talk to me? Because all I care about is getting Zach back here, safe."

"She really isn't here. She went out last night. I said I'd look after Zach. She was supposed to be back, but... well, she isn't."

"She's drinking," he said.

"That's unfair. You don't know that." In my mind, I was seeing Ronnie's face. I was seeing the way she had of looking up at me with her long-lashed eyes, her lips curved into a smile. "She just needed a break, okay? She was tired, and Zach was fussing. She just needed a bit of time to herself."

"Look, you don't have to tell me. I loved her. Still do, in a way." Max sounded tired and sad, more heartbroken than angry. "This is what she does. She'll be back eventually, in an hour or two, or a day or two, or a week. She'll apologize and she'll cry and she'll swear up and down that it'll never happen again. And you'll believe her, because it's so obvious that she means every word. And for a few weeks, everything will be fine. You'll think, maybe this time she'll keep it together, you know? But sooner or later…" I could almost hear his shrug over the phone. "It's why we split up."

I didn't know what to say. I didn't want to trust him, but there was something in his voice that told me he was telling the truth.

"So, where are you?" he asked. "I'll drive over and get Zach."

"We're in LA, actually."

There was a stunned silence. "Did you say LA? As in California? She took Zach to *California*?"

"Uh, yeah."

"She took him out of state. Damn." He sounded dazed. "I can't believe she took him out of state."

I felt guilty as hell. I'd been the one behind the wheel most of the way. "I had no idea," I say. "I mean, I thought she was a single mom, you know? I didn't mean to…well, to…"

"Help her kidnap my kid?"

"No. I mean, come on. It's not kidnapping. I mean, she is his mom."

"It's kidnapping," Max said. His voice was harsh. "Most kidnappings are committed by the noncustodial parent. Bet you didn't know that, huh?"

I could hardly breathe. "But she won't, you know, go to jail. Or stop being allowed to see Zach. Or..." My eyes were stinging.

He didn't reply right away, and when he did, his words didn't make me feel any better. "Where are you?" Max said. "Give me the address. I'm going to get the first flight I can."

Zach leaned his head back against my chest. I put my free hand on the top of his head and stroked his dark curls. His hair was feather-soft. I imagined how Ronnie must have felt, taking him home every Saturday evening and not seeing him all week.

I didn't agree with what she'd done, but I could see why she'd done it.

"Theo?" Max said. "I need the address."

I moved the phone away from my ear and stared at it. Just an ordinary white phone in a pink case, but I felt like I was holding a hand grenade. I just had to pull the pin and Ronnie's life would never be the same. I could hear Max's voice coming from the phone, low and urgent.

This was his kid sitting on my lap, I reminded myself. His kid. Not just Ronnie's.

I looked down at Zach. He had one fat fist clenched around a handful of raisins, as if he'd forgotten he had them. He looked a bit like Ronnie, with his long dark eyelashes and full lips. I took a deep breath, feeling torn. I wanted to do the right thing, but what the hell was that? Keeping Zach away from his father, who obviously adored him? Or letting Max know where Zach was—and getting Ronnie arrested for kidnapping?

It seemed to me that anything I did would be wrong. I didn't want to hurt anyone—there had already been enough damage done.

I guess it wasn't the smartest thing to do, but I just needed time to think.

So I hung up the phone.

It started to vibrate again immediately. I stood up, hoisted Zach onto my hip and dropped the phone back into Ronnie's bag. My mouth was dust-dry, but my hands were wet with sweat.

I had to talk to Ronnie. I had to make her see that she couldn't just run away from her problems. Maybe, if she called Max herself, she could explain. Make him understand, convince him not to take legal action…

A phone rang, and I almost jumped out of my skin before I realized that the ringing was coming from Joelle's room.

It wasn't Ronnie's phone. I should have known that, since hers was still set on vibrate. Then the ringing stopped and I heard Joelle's muffled voice. I blew out a long sigh of relief. "Maybe that's Ronnie, huh? Maybe she's calling Joelle to say she's on her way home." I sat back down in the chair with Zach, perching him on my knees and bouncing him up and down. "How about a horsey ride, kiddo? Bumpity-bump, bumpity-bump."

Zach gave a little squeal of delight. "Moh!"

"You want more? Okay! Bumpity-bump, bumpity-bump…"

Joelle stumbled out of her bedroom, wearing nothing but a tank top and underwear, bleary-eyed under a tousled mess of blond hair.

I stopped bumpity-bumping. "What is it? Was that Ronnie?"

"Max," she said. "That was Max. When you told him you guys were in

LA...well, I guess he figured Ronnie only had one friend down here."

"Oh crap. I didn't mean to..." I banged the heel of my hand against my forehead. I guess it was kind of a corny, melodramatic gesture, but it felt sort of good. I did it again, harder. "I didn't give him your address."

"Yeah. That'll take him about thirty seconds online." She shrugged, palms turned up in a what-can-you-do kind of gesture. "He's on his way. He'll be on the first flight he can catch."

Chapter Twelve

I hugged Zach so tight, he began to squirm. "What should we do?"

Joelle sighed. "Nothing. Wait, I guess." She picked a pair of flannel pants off the floor and pulled them on.

"Is Max an okay guy? I mean, was he abusive or anything like that?"

She gave me a puzzled look. "God, no. The guy was patient to a fault, you know? He stuck with her through all kinds of crap. I kept telling Ronnie, 'Don't screw this up.'" She shrugged. "Not that I'm saying it was all her fault that they split up. But…"

"She has a drinking problem," I said flatly.

Joelle bit her bottom lip. "I tried to tell you, but I didn't want to sound like I was bad-mouthing her, you know?"

"Yeah, I know." What was it about Ronnie that made us all want to protect her? It wasn't just that she was beautiful, or smart, or funny. There was something about her—a vulnerability, I guess. Maybe I was being sexist, but underneath the attitude and the independence, she seemed sort of fragile. "You said you guys go way back."

"We've been best friends since junior high. We played softball together. We were both total tomboys, if you can believe that."

"Seriously?" Back when Ronnie used to babysit me, she had long hair and wore tight T-shirts, tall leather boots and thick black eyeliner.

Joelle laughed. "We were twelve. It didn't last long." She stopped laughing abruptly and sat down on the arm of my chair. "How well did you know her?"

"Not at all, really." I looked down at Zach, who was unusually quiet. His eyes were half-closed. I lowered my voice, hoping he might drift off to sleep. "I was a kid, she was a teenager. Different worlds. She was nice to me. Took an interest in my projects, acted out *Star Wars* scenes with my action figures. I thought she was amazing, but I didn't know anything about her life."

"Her parents were alcoholics," Joelle said bluntly. "Both of them. Her dad put away a couple of martinis and a bottle of wine every night. His liver must be shot by now, but he had some big job and made tons of money. I don't think people outside the family even knew he had a problem."

"And her mom?"

"She drank like Ronnie does. Nothing at all for weeks, then she'd binge." Joelle shook her head. "Ronnie never talked about it, but I remember going over to her place after school one day. Her mom was completely out of it, stumbling around the house and shouting at Ronnie, trying to hit her, calling her really foul names. We were fourteen, I guess. It was awful."

"It sounds like it." Lately, I'd been giving my parents a hard time about their daily happy hour, but my objections seemed kind of petty now. Sure, it was annoying that they thought a daily drink was fine while Koli's smoking pot was apparently the end of the world—but to be fair, I'd never seen either of them have more than two drinks. I'd never seen them drunk.

"Yeah. My mom said Ronnie could stay with us anytime. Ronnie was mad that I had told, but after that she did stay with us a lot." Joelle shrugged. "Then when we were sixteen, Ronnie's dad got transferred and they moved to Seattle. I think things with her family went downhill after that."

"Didn't sound like it could get much worse," I said.

"No kidding." Joelle leaned toward me. "Zach's out cold. You want to put him down on my bed?"

I nodded, stood up with him in my arms and carried him into her room. Joelle pushed the covers to one side and I put Zach down in the middle of her bed, with pillows on both sides so he wouldn't roll off. His eyelashes were dark spiky lines against his flushed cheeks. He looked perfect. Everything was still possible for him, I thought, if only the adults in his life didn't screw it all up.

"He's pretty sweet," Joelle said.

"Yeah. Especially when he's sleeping." I followed Joelle back out to the living room, still thinking about what she had said. "So if Max shows up, we just give Zach to him?"

"Yeah, I guess. I mean, Ronnie's not here, is she? And I can't look after her kid. Besides, Max has custody. Did Ronnie tell you that?"

"No. Max did though."

"I couldn't have ratted on Ronnie to him, but honestly, Theo, this is probably a good thing. He's a lot more stable than she is. I mean, she's a good mom in lots of ways, and she adores Zach, but if she keeps coming apart like this, how can she take care of a kid?"

"Yeah. I get it."

She yawned. "I'm sorry, but I've got to crash. I'm going to join Zach, okay?

Wake me up if…well, if Ronnie shows up, I guess."

"Okay." I wasn't sure what to hope for. I couldn't imagine just handing Zach over to his dad without even talking to Ronnie, but on the other hand, how was I going to tell her what I had done?

I flopped back into the armchair and closed my eyes. My whole body ached with tiredness. I'd slept last night, but not well, and I'd been up driving right through the night before. Still, it wasn't the lack of sleep that was making me feel like I'd been hit by a truck. It was Ronnie.

How could I be so crazy about her and so angry with her at the same time? And how could she be so perfect and such a mess? I found myself remembering what she'd said as we drove into LA, something about polluted cities having the best sunrises. She was kind of like this city, in a way. So much glamour and gorgeousness, yet, underneath it, so much desperation.

I should call my parents, I thought tiredly. Let them know I wouldn't be getting on the bus this morning. They'd argue, but I wasn't too worried about that. My problems with my parents felt so distant from the mess I was dealing with here—and so trivial compared to what Ronnie had run away from. When I got home, things would be different. Darrell was right—I couldn't change them, so I'd just have to learn not to take it all so personally. The way forward didn't seem half as complicated as the miles behind us. After all, there were worse things than having your parents worry about you.

I yawned so widely that my jaw cracked. In a minute, I'd call. In a minute...

Chapter Thirteen

I must have dozed off, because the next thing I knew, the living-room door slammed and then Ronnie was standing in front of me, her dark hair wild and uncombed, her mascara smudged under her eyes. "Where's Zach? Is he okay?"

I struggled to get up. "Fine. He's asleep in Joelle's room." I caught her arm. "Don't go in there. Joelle's sleeping too. Besides, we need to talk."

"I know." A tear traced a pale path through her ruined makeup. "I'm so sorry, Theo. I'm really, really sorry. I didn't mean to be gone so long. Honestly, I was only going to take a little break. But…"

"But then you started drinking." If I'd had any doubts, they were gone now. I could hear the slur in her speech. I could smell the booze and the cigarettes on her breath.

"I'm sorry." She gave a hiccupping kind of sob. "I'm such a goddamn mess, Theo."

I had to tell her that Max was on his way. She was going to hate me, but I had to tell her. "You didn't drive home, did you?"

She shook her head. "I left the car somewhere. Took a cab home. Cost me twenty bucks."

"Well, that was a good decision anyway."

"I'm not a total idiot, you know."

"I don't think you're an idiot at all," I said. "You're just unhappy." I studied her face—her blue eyes, so like Zach's with their thick fringe of lashes, her straight dark eyebrows, the soft curve of her cheeks. I swallowed hard, and my throat ached with the effort of holding back my own tears. "I...uh...Ronnie, you know I really care about you. I wish I could fix things for you."

"You can't," she said. "No one can." She started to cry for real, and I held out my arms. She leaned against me, her head on my shoulder. I rested my chin on the top of her head and stroked her hair. "I've messed everything up," she whispered. "I always do."

I had to tell her. It'd be awful if Max just arrived and she didn't know. "Ronnie," I said. "Please don't hate me.

But…well, when you didn't come home, I looked at the messages on your phone. I talked to Max."

I felt her whole body go still, as if she had stopped even breathing. Then she let out a long shuddering gasp. "So you know then. You know what I did."

"I know Max has custody of Zach. Yeah."

"Is he coming to get him?" She pulled back, looked at me and wiped the tears from her cheeks. "He is, isn't he?"

I nodded. "Ronnie, you have to talk to him."

"He'll be furious," she said. "He'll hate me."

"He doesn't hate you," I said. "I could tell. He was upset and worried, but he definitely doesn't hate you."

"He should then," Ronnie said. "I hate myself."

She was standing right in front of me, but I felt like there was a thick glass wall between us, like nothing I said would reach her. "Don't say that, Ronnie."

"It's the truth."

I hesitated, not wanting to say anything that would make her feel worse. "Look, Joelle told me a bit about your family. It sounds like you've had some lousy stuff to deal with. So don't be so hard on yourself."

"I used to be so sure I'd never be like them," she said. "I didn't drink at all when I was pregnant, you know. Not once. And when Zach was born, I promised him I'd be such a good mother."

I wanted to tell her she was a good mother, but I couldn't bring myself to say it. "You love him," I said instead. "That's why you did this, right?"

"Of course I *love* him," she said. "But that's not enough, is it? Anyway, that's not really why I took him. Or not the whole reason anyway."

"So why did you do it then?"

She sighed. "I just thought…I thought if I had him with me, I wouldn't keep doing this shit. Drinking, I mean. I thought I could do it for him, you know?"

"Maybe you should get some help," I said. "Go to an AA meeting, or talk to a counselor or something."

She folded her arms across her chest, her hands gripping her shoulders so tightly, her knuckles were turning white— like she was literally trying to hold herself together. "I'll figure it out," she said.

"You don't have to do it on your own, you know."

"Yeah," she said. "I do."

Ultimately, I guessed, that was true. No one could do it for her. Still, she had friends. "Listen, Joelle told me to wake her if you came back."

"No, let her sleep. I want to see Zach though." She disappeared into Joelle's bedroom and came back a minute later with Zach, still fast asleep, in her arms.

"Here, sit down." I gestured to the chair. It had just occurred to me that Ronnie could take off again, taking Zach with her, and how would I stop her?

Ronnie sat down and settled Zach on her lap, his head against her chest. "I'll miss him so much," she said, stroking his hair. "I can't believe this is happening."

"You can still see him on weekends, right?"

"After this? Who knows."

"Talk to Max," I said. "Seriously. I could tell he still cares about you."

"I don't deserve it," she said.

"Yeah, Ronnie. You do. You deserve way more than you've had." My voice cracked. "I care about you too."

She gave me a smile. Then, to my surprise, she laughed. "But that's Luke's line, isn't it?"

"What are you talking about? Luke who?"

"Skywalker, goof. Leia says, *I wonder if Han really cares about anyone*. And Luke says, *I care*."

I stared at her. "I can't believe you remember that."

"Come on, you made me act out that whole movie about a million times. It's permanently carved into my memory."

"Wow." I shook my head. "Well, for what it's worth, I do care."

"You're a good kid, Theo."

I shook my head. "I'm not a kid anymore, Ronnie."

"I know you're not." She stood up. "Take Zach, okay? I'm not going to wait for Max. Would you look after Zach until he gets here?"

"But—"

"Please?"

I took Zach from her. For some reason, the warmth of his body and the weight of him in my arms made me want to cry. "Ronnie, are you sure?"

"I need to do this on my own." She met my eyes. "Tell Joelle thanks. I left her spare key on her bedside table. And tell Max I'm sorry. Tell him...tell him I'm taking some time to myself. To sort myself out, you know?"

"You could do that in Seattle," I said. "And that way you could still see Zach on the weekends."

"I can't do it in Seattle," she said. "I already tried doing it in Seattle. That's why I came here."

"Yeah, but that didn't work, did it? Maybe it wasn't Seattle that was the problem." Zach stirred in my arms, and I lowered my voice. "Look, I was running away from problems too. That's why I came here with you. But I think...well, maybe you need to stop running. Face the music." I winced. "Sorry. *Face the music*. That's something my mom's always saying. I can't believe I just said it."

"Well, maybe your mom's right. But I

131

don't think I can do it." Ronnie stood up. "Thanks for everything, Theo."

"Don't go." I stood there, holding her child, while Ronnie turned and walked out the door.

Then I sank down into the armchair.

I'd failed.

Ronnie was still running away, looking for a city or a place or a person who would make everything okay—and I was going to have to explain it all to Max. I hoped I could persuade him not to pursue any kind of legal action, at least. I had a feeling he wouldn't want to, once he had Zach safely home again.

I looked down at Zach. The apartment was hot. His hair was damp and sticking to his forehead, and his cheeks were flushed. I thought of Ronnie promising him she'd be a good mother, and I couldn't help wondering if her own mother had ever made that same promise. Whether she had or not, she'd done a lot of damage.

I knew Ronnie loved Zach, but sometimes love and good intentions just weren't enough. I didn't think she'd be able to fix anything if she couldn't stay in one place and face what was wrong.

Time passed. Half an hour. An hour. I wondered when Zach would wake up. I wondered when Max would arrive. I thought about my parents, and how things were going to be different from here on in, and—

A knock at the front door sent a jolt of adrenaline flooding through me. *Max*. I stood, carried Zach across the room and opened the door.

And there was Ronnie.

"You came back," I said.

"I was waiting at the bus stop, and the bus came and, well, I just didn't get on it." She lifted her chin and gave me a smile that just about broke my heart. It was so brave and so…well, so *Ronnie*. "You're right," she said. "It's time to stop running."

Acknowledgments

Many thanks to family and friends who helped me with this book, especially my writing buddy Alex Van Tol for great company and fabulous suggestions. Thanks also to Andrew Wooldridge and the wonderful Orca pod.

About the Author

Robin Stevenson is the author of more than a dozen books for children, teens and young adults. *Damage* is Robin's fourth book in the Orca Soundings series, following *Big Guy, In the Woods* and *Outback*. Her other novels for teens include the Governor General's Literary Award nominee *A Thousand Shades of Blue*, as well as *Inferno, Out of Order, Escape Velocity* and *Hummingbird Heart*. Robin lives in Victoria, BC. For more information, visit her website: www.robinstevenson.com.